This LADYBIRD TALE
belongs to

....

The Gingerbread Man

Retold by Vera Southgate M.A., B.COM
with illustrations by Daniel Howarth

LADYBIRD 🐞 TALES

ONCE UPON A TIME there was a little old woman and a little old man. They lived by themselves in a little old house.

They had no little boys and no little girls.

One day, the little old woman said
to the little old man, "I shall make
a little boy out of gingerbread.
I shall make his eyes from two
fat currants. I shall make his nose
and mouth from bits of lemon peel.
I shall make his coat from sugar."

So the little old woman mixed
the gingerbread. She cut out the
little boy's head, his body, his arms
and his legs. She patted them out
flat on a baking tin.

Then the little old woman gave him
two fat currants for his eyes. For
his nose and mouth she gave him
two bits of lemon peel.

She made his coat from sugar.

The little old woman put the gingerbread boy into the oven to bake.

"Oh-ho!" she cried. "Now I shall have a little gingerbread boy of my own."

Then she went about her work.

Soon it was time for the little
gingerbread boy to be ready.

As the little old woman went
to the oven, she heard a tiny little
voice crying, "Let me out! Let
me out!"

Then the little old woman ran
to open the oven door. As she
did so, out popped the little
gingerbread boy.

The little gingerbread boy hopped and skipped across the kitchen floor.

He saw the door of the kitchen standing open and out he ran.

Down the street ran the little gingerbread boy. After him ran the little old woman and the little old man.

"Stop, stop, little gingerbread boy!" they cried.

But the little gingerbread boy only looked back and cried,

"Run, run, as fast as you can,
You can't catch me,
I'm the gingerbread man!"

And they could not catch him.

The little gingerbread boy ran on and on. Soon he met a cow.

"Stop, stop, little gingerbread boy!" said the cow. "You look very good to eat."

But the little gingerbread boy only ran faster.

"I have run away from a little old
woman and a little old man,"
cried the little gingerbread boy.
"I can run away from you, too.

Run, run, as fast as you can,
You can't catch me,
I'm the gingerbread man!"

And the cow could not catch him.

The little gingerbread boy ran on
and on. Soon he met a horse.

"Stop, stop, little gingerbread boy!"
said the horse. "You look very good
to eat."

But the little gingerbread boy only
ran faster.

"I have run away from a little
old woman, a little old man and
a cow," cried the little gingerbread
boy. "I can run away from you, too.

Run, run, as fast as you can,
You can't catch me,
I'm the gingerbread man!"

And the horse could not catch him.

The little gingerbread boy ran on and on. He began to feel very proud of his running. "No one can catch me," he said.

Just then he met a sly old fox.

"Stop, stop, little gingerbread boy!" said the fox. "I want to talk to you."

"Oh-ho! You can't catch me!" said the little gingerbread boy and he began to run faster.

The fox began to run after the little gingerbread boy. The little gingerbread boy began to run faster still.

As he ran, the little gingerbread boy looked back and cried, "I have run away from a little old woman, a little old man, a cow and a horse. I can run away from you, too.

Run, run, as fast as you can,
You can't catch me,
I'm the gingerbread man!"

"I don't want to catch you," said the sly old fox. "I just want to talk to you."

But the little gingerbread boy kept on running. And the fox kept on running.

Soon the little gingerbread boy came to a river. He stopped at the riverbank and the fox came running up.

"Oh! What shall I do?" cried the little gingerbread boy. "I cannot cross the river."

"Jump onto my tail," said the sly old fox, "and I will take you across the river."

So the little gingerbread boy jumped onto the fox's tail.

The fox began to swim across the river.

Soon the sly old fox turned his head and said, "Little gingerbread boy, you are too heavy for my tail. You will get wet. Jump up onto my back."

So the little gingerbread boy jumped onto the fox's back.

The sly old fox swam a little further out into the river.

Then he turned his head again and said, "Little gingerbread boy, you are too heavy for my back. You will get wet. Jump onto my nose."

So the little gingerbread boy jumped onto the fox's nose.

Soon the fox reached the other side of the river. As soon as his feet touched the bank of the river, he tossed the gingerbread boy into the air.

The fox opened his mouth and – SNAP! – went his teeth.

"Oh dear!" said the little gingerbread boy. "I am one-quarter gone!"

Then he cried, "I am half gone!"

Then he cried, "I am three-quarters gone!"

After that, the little gingerbread boy said nothing more at all.

A History of
The Gingerbread Man

The Gingerbread Man character has appeared in films, TV programmes, songs and novels. The tale's widespread success is probably down to its simple rhythm and rhyme and its popularity as a nursery story.

The exact origins of the story of *The Gingerbread Man* are unknown. Norwegian writers Peter Christen Asbjørnsen and Jørgen Moe wrote an early version which appeared in the mid-1800s, called *The Pancake*. A later adaptation, *The Fleeing Pancake*, became the most popular version in Europe.

The Gingerbread Man made his first appearance in the May 1875 issue of *St. Nicholas* magazine, but children were already familiar with the story by that time. The simple tale has inspired many modern runaway food tales, including Ying Chang Compestine's Chinese New Year tale, *The Runaway Rice Cake.*

Collect more fantastic
LADYBIRD 🐞 TALES

9781409311072

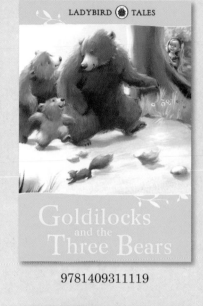

9781409311119

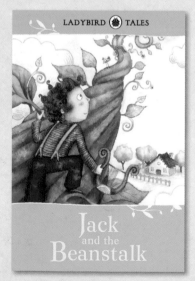

9781409311102

9781409311126

The Gingerbread Man

9781409311096

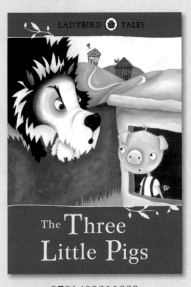

The Three Little Pigs

9781409311089

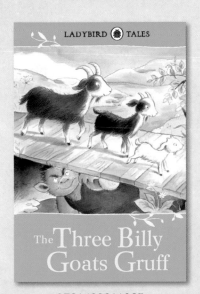

The Three Billy Goats Gruff

9781409311065

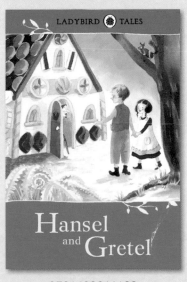

Hansel and Gretel

9781409311133

Endpapers taken from series 606d,
first published in 1964

A catalogue record for this book is available from the British Library

Published by Ladybird Books Ltd
80 Strand London WC2R 0RL
A Penguin Company

007

ISBN: 978-1-40931-109-6

Printed in China